The Frog Prince

To Katherine

Samuel Valentino

Written and illustrated by

Samuel Valentino

© 2015 by Samuel Valentino

All rights reserved. Published by Brattle Publishing Group, LLC.
www.brattlepublishing.com

No part of this publication may be reproduced, stored in a retrieval system,or transmitted
in any form or by any means, electronic, mechanical, photocopying, recording,
or otherwise, without written permission of the publisher.

For information regarding permission, write to:

Brattle Publishing Group
Attention: Permissions
info@brattlepublishing.com

Library of Congress Cataloging-in-Publication Data is available

ISBN 13: 978-0-9854295-6-0

ISBN 10: 0985429569

Printed in the United States of America
First edition, January 2015

Version: 2014.12.17

To the real Princess Moy Moy
Arianna (aka Rocket)

Once there was a beautiful princess named Moy Moy.

Every day she played in the castle gardens with her golden ball.

Just then, a frog popped his head out of the water.

"I'll get your ball back for you," he said.

"But only if," he added . . .

"... you promise to share your table . . ."

"... and share your food . . ."

"... and share your cup . . ."

"... and share your pillow with me."

So the frog got the golden ball for her.

**Princess Moy Moy was so excited that
she ran back to the castle without the frog.**

At dinnertime, there was a knock on the door.

"But you promised," said the frog.

"But you promised," said the frog.

"Yes, I did,"
she sighed.
So the frog
shared her food.

"Yes, I did," she sighed.
So the frog shared her cup.

"Yes, I did," she sighed.
So the frog shared her pillow.

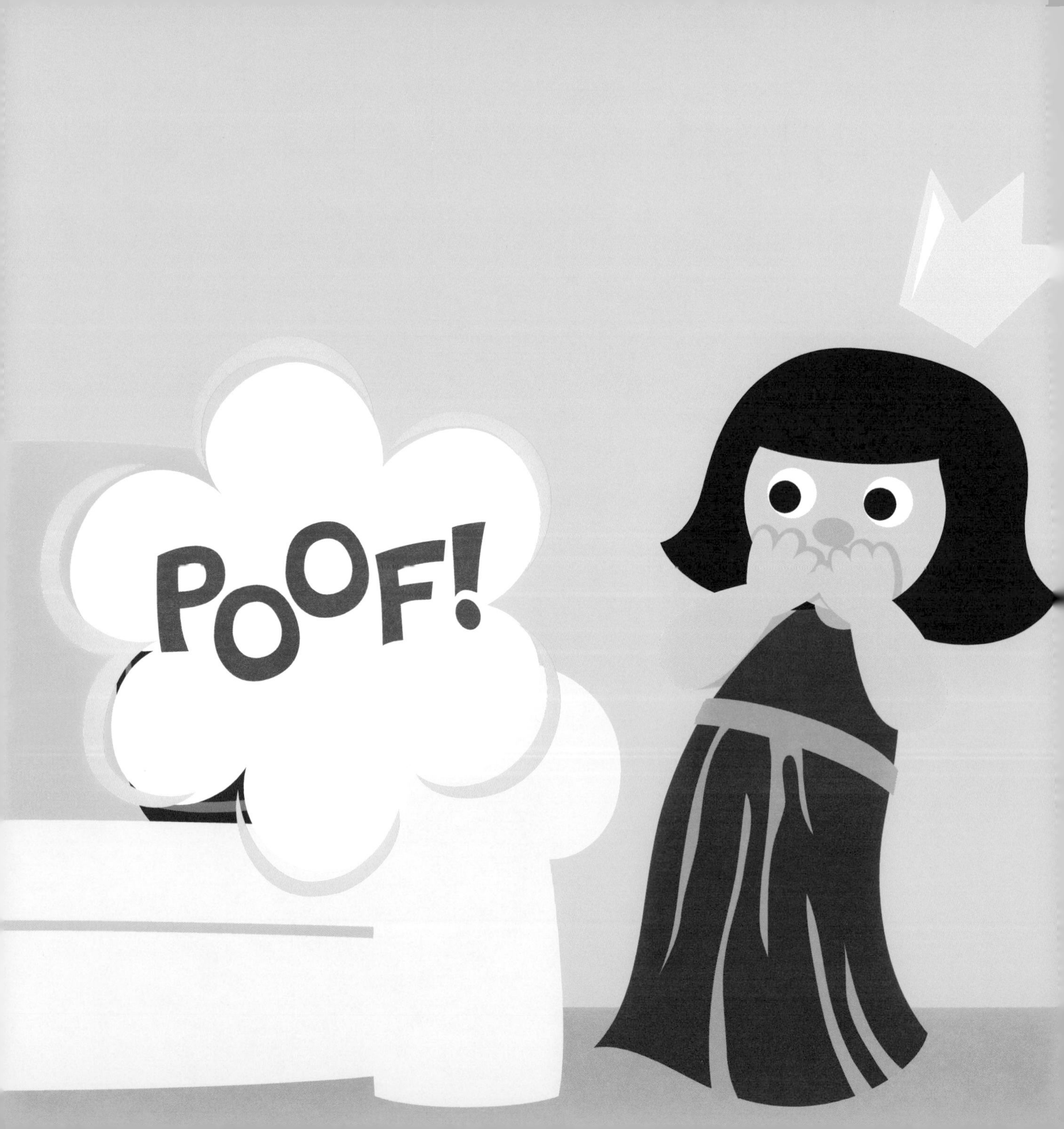
POOF!

The frog changed into a prince!
"I am a prince again because I found
someone who can share!" he said.

And Princess Moy Moy and the Prince were very happy.

CPSIA information can be obtained at www.ICGtesting.com
Printed in the USA
BVIW12n1355180115
383742BV00001B/1